D1034654

SWIMMER'S MARK

BY
EVELYN LUNEMANN

ILLUSTRATIONS BY
KENNETH M. SHIELDS

BENEFIC PRESS • WESTCHESTER, ILLINOIS

SPORTS MYSTERY SERIES

TEN FEET TALL

NO TURNING BACK

FAIRWAY DANGER

TIP OFF

PITCHER'S CHOICE

FACE-OFF

SWIMMER'S MARK

TENNIS CHAMP

Library of Congress
Number 70-184268

Printed in the United States of America

CONTENTS

Not Like Others

Felix Ruben sang loudly as the water from the shower ran over his body. "Uummmmm!" he sighed. "Water! I love it. I could stay here all day." He lifted his face to catch the full force of the spray. "La De La Da Dumm." He sang at the top of his voice.

"I suppose I can't stay here forever," he thought. "The world needs me." With a quick push Felix turned the water off. He reached out for the towel. Suddenly his hand stopped in midair. He turned his head to one side and listened. The noise of the running water had kept him from hearing the sound which now reached his ears. Yes, the sound was coming from his sister's room. Felix shook his head. "She's crying, all right," he said to himself.

"Girls!" said Felix as he dried himself. "No, " he thought. "That's not quite fair. Sarah has a lot to cry about."

Felix took only a minute to slip on his robe, then hurried quickly down the hallway. "Sarah!" He stood outside the door to his sister's room. There was no answer. "Sarah, open the door," he called again. Still there was no answer. "Open the door, Sarah." He listened with his ear to the door. "I'm coming in," he announced. The sound of sobs was the only thing he heard. "Here I come," he said, and opened the door.

Sarah lay huddled on her bed. Her whole body seemed to shake as she tried to stop crying. Felix reached to touch the dark hair that was so much like his own. Then with a shake of his head he drew his hand back. He ran his hand through his own hair. Drops of water flew as he stood there, not knowing what to say.

Felix thought to himself, "I'll bet I can just about guess what's wrong with her. But what can I say?" For a moment he thought about his mother and father. They were good parents, but they believed in doing things the "old way." The old way was pretty hard on a young girl.

"Come on, Sarah," Felix said kindly. "Whatever it is, crying isn't going to help. Besides, it's almost time for you to go to work."

"Oh, no!" Sarah wailed. She scrambled from the bed. "It is time," she said as she looked at the clock. Her hands flew to her hair. "My hair!" she sobbed. "Look at it. What will I do?" She stared at herself in the mirror. "Just look at me!" she cried as she began to comb her hair. "And I'll have to soak my eyes in cold water. Will you please give me a ride to The Del, Felix?"

"All right, but hurry," Felix answered. "I'm supposed to be at swim practice in a few minutes."

Felix shook his head and smiled as he made his way to his own room. Girls were mighty strange. One minute they could feel one way and then— Bang— they could change just like that!

Sarah dressed quickly. She must not be late for work. Besides, she liked to work at The Del. Her father and mother ran this favorite eating-place for the young people of the city. She loved the spicy smell of the corned beef and big dill pickles. She liked to be where activity was always going on. There was something about working at The Del that made her feel a part of all the young people's activities.

"My eyes aren't too bad," she thought. She pinned a small cap on her head. "Maybe by the time I get there I'll look all right."

"Let's go," called Felix.

"I'm coming," answered Sarah. She ran for the front door.

"What started the trouble this time?" Felix asked his sister as she jumped into the seat beside him.

"Oh, I asked if I could go to The Center mixer with Mike Fisher. Of course Mom and Dad both said 'No'." Sarah pulled down the car mirror and began to check her hair.

"I don't know what to say," Felix said. "If they'd let you go with anyone, it would be Mike."

"I'm going," Sarah said matter-of-factly. "I don't know how I'm going to get them to change their minds. All I know is that I'm going to that mixer with Mike. Nobody is going to stop me."

Felix turned to look closely at his sister. He had never seen her act quite like this before.

"Felix, I'm only a year younger than you are," Sarah went on. "You went to the mixer when you were my age. It's just not fair."

"I guess the difference is that I didn't take a girl," Felix said.

"I can't very well go by myself—or even with Mary. Mom and Dad would never stand for that." Sarah set her chin in a firm line. "No," she said, "I'm going with Mike."

"All I can say is, good luck. If I get a chance to say anything to Mom and Dad, I will. It's not likely to do any good, though." Felix stopped the car in front of The Del.

"Thanks," Sarah smiled at her brother. "Thanks for the ride, too. See you later." She hopped out of the car and went into The Del.

Felix took a deep breath as he drove on toward The Center, where the city's outdoor pool was located. "Now for my own problems," he thought. Maybe things were easier for Sarah than for himself, after all.

There it was again—that old tight feeling in his chest. It came every time Felix thought about the State Swim Meet to be held in a few short weeks.

Felix liked swimming and he worked hard at it. The butterfly was the stroke in which he did his best work. His time in the 100-yard butterfly had not improved for what seemed like a long time. If he did not break a minute soon, there would be no use in planning to go to the State Meet. Felix still remembered the results of the last time trials.

100-yard Butterfly

Zapp	0:59.9
Budd	1:01
Ruben	1:03

"What's the matter with me?" he asked himself. "Why can't I cut my time down? I know there are times when one doesn't get better, but this has gone on for such a long time."

Felix was still troubled as he parked the car in The Center lot. An old feeling returned to hurt him. Why was it that so often he found himself going to practice alone? Most of the other boys arrived in pairs or groups. The other fellows seemed to like him. He could talk and joke with anyone. But somehow he often felt as though he were on the outside looking in.

"Hi, fellows," Felix called to several boys who had jumped out of a car. The boys turned and gave him a half-hearted wave. They did not stop or even slow their walk to wait for him. Felix hurried to catch them.

"Hi," he said again.

One of the young men stopped and turned to look at Felix. "Oh, hello, Felix," he said. The young man was Mike Fisher. The other boys walked through the gate and into The Center.

Felix smiled. Then an old thought returned to nag him. "Mike waits for me because he likes my sister." He felt ashamed as soon as the thought came to his mind. "That's not true," Felix told himself. "Mike is my friend."

"How's everything?" asked Mike.

"Fine, I think," Felix answered as he walked beside Mike. It was good to be with his friend. "It's so hot. The water is going to feel good."

"I know what you mean," Mike agreed. "It sure was hot at work today."

"I have to go to work at The Del after practice," Felix told Mike.

"I'll ride with you if that's all right," said Mike.

"Sure thing," Felix answered.

"I wonder if Coach is going to time us today," asked Mike.

"I'm afraid so," Felix said. "Might as well get the bad news now as later." Felix tried to make his voice sound light and happy. "You don't have to worry, Mike. With your time in the 100-yard freestyle, you would be able to do well in any meet we have around here."

"I don't know," said Mike. "I can't seem to bring my time down enough."

"You!" exploded Felix. "I'm the one with that problem. Do you know how long I've been trying to break a minute in that 100-yard butterfly? I don't know why I can't. I feel that I can do it and then in the last few yards something happens to slow me down."

"Maybe this will be the day," Mike told him. "Remember what Coach says: 'You have to believe that you can do it.' "

"My mind says that I can do it," answered Felix, "but sometimes the rest of me doesn't seem to get the message."

"I know what you mean," laughed Mike.

Mike and Felix made their way into the dressing room. They heard the boys laughing as though someone had just told a good joke. "What's so funny?" asked Mike.

"We were just talking about last year when we were at the State Swim Meet," the swimmer Zapp replied. "Remember how Felix got locked in the bathroom of our hotel?"

"Yeh," added another young man named Budd. "He had all that time and he didn't even get the curls combed out of his hair."

"Don't forget to tell how I slept on the floor because of Zapp's big feet. Those feet of his took up all the room in the bed," Felix teased back at them.

A long time ago Felix had learned to tell a joke on himself before someone else did. He knew that the boys liked the way he could laugh at himself. Only sometimes Felix had to laugh at himself when he didn't feel there was anything funny. Felix remembered that meet very well. He had gone as the team manager. The trip had been fun, but Felix had not felt as if he were really a part of the team.

Zapp sat with his bare feet pushed out in front of him. "Be careful how you talk about my beautiful big feet," he told the group.

"Remember the time we were going to throw Felix in the pool at the motel?" asked Budd.

"Yes, with my clothes on," added Felix.

"There was only one thing that saved him," Budd went on.

"Tell us," begged one of the newer members of the team.

There were loud laughs from some of the boys as they thought of the fun of the year before.

"There we were, swinging him out over the water. Then he told us he had his money in a belt around his waist. We knew that with all the money he has, he'd be sure to sink if we threw him in." Budd laughed as he remembered.

"Of course, the fact that Coach came along had nothing to do with your deciding not to throw me in," said Felix.

Just then Coach Burton walked into the dressing room. "All right, men," he said. "Let's not take all day in here. We have a lot of work to do. We'll do a few lengths and then some time trials."

"A few lengths," muttered Zapp. "Coach doesn't know the meaning of a few. He means a few dozen."

"I heard that," announced the coach. "Just a few wiggles of those big feet is all I ask."

"OK, OK, Coach. I'm coming," answered Zapp. He headed for the door to the pool.

There was the sound of locker doors being slammed. Bare feet slapped across the tile floor as the boys hurried from the room.

Soon the pool was full of splashes as, one after another, the swimmers dived into the water. Some of the boys used kick-boards as they did their lengths. Others swam relay-style in order to make room for more swimmers in the pool.

The coach seemed to be everywhere at once. As he walked up and down the side of the pool, he had a word for each swimmer. Most of the time his words were meant to make the work more fun. Sometimes he spoke sharply to a lazy swimmer.

Even the tightness that Felix felt about the time trials could not take away the good feeling that the water gave to him. He felt the cool water close over him and thought, "It's good. The water is good." Somehow it seemed to wash all his troubles away—at least for a little while.

The shrill sound of the coach's whistle came to Felix's ears. "Everybody out!" shouted the coach. "Come on. Let's get some times." He handed the stopwatches to the boys who were not going to be in the first races. "Remember how I told you to use those watches. Get the split-times, too."

Felix watched as Mike swam the 100-yard freestyle in a near record-breaking time. Mike was overjoyed as he pulled himself from the water.

"What were you saying about bringing your time down?" Felix asked Mike as he patted his friend on the back.

"You butterfly men get ready," called the coach. "Zapp, take lane 5. Budd, lane 6. Ruben, lane 4. Green, you take lane 3. Now watch your starts. Really stretch out. Get everything you can out of your glide. Zapp, don't jump the gun. False starts don't help anyone. Ruben, watch your breathing. Green, you show these fellows how it should be done."

"On your marks!" yelled Coach Burton. Felix bent low over the water. His eyes stared at the far end. "I can do it, I can do it," he said over and over. For a moment he was afraid he was going to fall forward. Bang! sounded the gun.

There was a part of a second when all the swimmers were stretched out over the water. Then the four hit the water with the loud smacks of the racing dives.

"Use your glide," Felix told himself. He could feel that he had made a good start.

The pulling arms and the dolphin kicks churned the water.

"Don't think," Felix said to himself. "Just swim. Breathe. Pull. Pull. Pace yourself." The thoughts still raced through his mind. "Save time for the finish. Pull. Pull."

As he made the turn at the far end, he heard someone yelling at him. He heard no words, only the sound of a voice, as if from a far distance.

"Where are Zapp or Budd?" he thought. "Don't look. Takes time." Then the names began to ring in his head. "Zapp, Budd. Zapp. Budd." His eyes saw a froth of water ahead of him. Zapp was leading. "Now for the last spurt. Pull." His arms felt as if they were sticks of heavy wood. "I'm coming too far out of the water," he told himself. His body seemed not to move. "I've done it again. There's no energy left for the finish of the race."

The wall. Suddenly it was there. Felix clung to its hard edge. His heart pounded. There was no need to look around. He knew that Zapp and Budd had finished ahead of him.

Mike was leaning over him. "Good going, Felix. It's your best time yet. One minute."

Felix heard no more of what Mike said. It was his best time, but it wasn't good enough. His chest heaved, but he managed to ask, "What did Zapp get?"

"59.7," Mike answered.

"It's what I expected," thought Felix. He turned his head and saw Green coming to the finish line. All too well, Felix remembered how it felt to be last. As Green touched the wall, Felix said, "Nice going, Green." Green's eyes answered him. Felix knew that Green was too tired even to say, "Thanks."

"Nice going," Felix said to Zapp. He lay back in the water, eyes closed, relaxing.

"Each one of you brought your time down," Coach Burton said to them. "That's great, men. Felix, what happened? You had plenty left at the finish. Why didn't you use it?"

Felix shook his head as he pulled himself out of the water. He reached for his towel and sweat shirt. Something about the feel of the shirt comforted him. He sat down on the bench beside Green. Green had his head in his hands. "Feel sick?" asked Felix. Green nodded. "It won't last long," promised Felix. "I've had that feeling a few times myself."

The next event was the 400-yard freestyle. The coach came to stand beside Felix as he waited for the race to finish.

"You're pulling that time down, Felix. Do you know your split-time was better than Zapp's? You didn't even look tired near the finish. You can do better, though. I'm sure of it. Sometimes this swimming is a thinking game. You're going to have to 'think' yourself across those last few yards."

Felix nodded his head. What the coach was saying was true. He knew that he could do better.

"The main thing is that you've brought your time down. You'll break a minute before the Meet." Coach Burton patted Felix on the shoulder.

Felix had no more time to think about himself. He was kept busy timing the remaining races. When all of the trials were over, Coach Burton waved the boys to the far end of the pool.

"I'm proud of you as a team," he said. "Most of you have really worked hard. A few of you could do a whole lot better if you'd get to bed at a decent hour. Unless you want to stay in training, you may as well quit. The rest of you have done a fine job. We'll have another time trial before the Meet. We have a chance of taking some firsts and seconds. Besides, we have a lot of depth that will help us. I can't think of a team that can beat us—if we keep on improving." The coach walked back and forth in front of the boys. When he stopped and looked at them, his face was troubled.

"I'm afraid I have some bad news, men." His eyes seemed to look at each boy in turn. "What you do about it will, as they say, 'separate the men from the boys.' If you're men, you'll keep on working hard. If you're not, there isn't much anyone can do to help you. The truth is, we have a problem. The Center Office has just told me that they do not have enough money to pay our way to the State Meet. Time is short. It's too bad we didn't learn about this before."

For a minute there was no sound from the boys. The day had not seemed chilly before. Now some of them shivered.

"How much do we need?" asked one of the boys.

"That depends on how many men we send. If we can't get enough money to send the whole team, it means that only the top swimmers will go. We'll take the men we can use in more than one race."

"Couldn't we each pay our own way?" Zapp asked.

Everyone knew that Zapp was one of the few boys who would have no trouble in getting enough money. All eyes turned toward Zapp.

"No!" The word was almost like a shout as Coach Burton answered Zapp.

"Well, I only thought. . ." said Zapp.

"No," said Coach Burton again. "We're going with money on hand for everyone or we aren't going. The ones who go will be those who have worked hardest on swimming. It won't be the ones who have the most money."

"Maybe we could earn the money," said Mike.

"Yes, I think we could. I don't know just how—yet," the coach said carefully. "I want each of you to go home and put your mind to work. We ought to be able to come up with something. There is one thing. If you decide to earn the money, it may mean that some of you will help earn money and not get a chance to go. You must understand."

"Now comes the hard part," went on Coach Burton. "If you think you are going to slack up on practice, you're wrong. If you're men, this problem ought to make you just that much tougher. Somehow, I think we'll find a way out of our trouble. I hope so. In the meantime, we're going to practice harder than ever. Now get in that water. Do more lengths than you've ever done. When you're sure you can't do any more, then do a few more and a few more after that."

For a minute the boys sat still. Then Felix bounded from the bench. "What are we waiting for?" he yelled.

Before Felix hit the water, others followed. There was little talk as the boys fell to practicing.

Coach Burton sat down on the bench and smiled to himself as he watched. "Kids," he said aloud. "You can't beat them."

Problems! Problems!

Mike and Felix said little on their way to The Del. After practice Felix usually felt tired, but ready to face the world. Today he felt only tired. There was one thought he could not push from his mind. "What if I can't go to the Meet?" Zapp and Budd could both swim well in other strokes. Felix had only his butterfly. Surely the coach would not take him if only the top swimmers were going. Last year he had gone as the team manager. He had not swum at all. "I have to break a minute," he told himself over and over. "I can't stand to think about not going to the Meet."

All of the reasons why he wanted to go to the Meet came rushing into Felix's mind. First, there were his father and mother. They were proud to have him swimming on the team. He knew that it cost them time and money every time he went to practice. Then there was Sarah. More than once Sarah had told him how great it made her feel to have him on the swim team. Most of all, Felix had never felt as much a part of the crowd as he had since becoming a team member.

"Oh, I could eat everything in sight," sighed Mike as Felix stopped the car in front of The Del. Mike threw back his head and sniffed. "Mmm," he said. "Lead me to it."

Sarah and Mike's sister Mary were working behind the counter as Felix and Mike entered the cafe. Felix went behind the counter and put on an apron. "What will it be?" he asked Mike. Sarah was beside the two boys before Mike could answer.

"Never mind," she told Felix. "I'll wait on Mike."

Felix smiled. "I'll wait on myself, then. As soon as I have something to eat, I'll help you with the customers."

The door to the kitchen opened. Mr. Ruben made his way carefully through the doorway. He was a tall man and quite heavy. He arms were loaded with a tray of meat and cheese. A big smile covered his face as he saw the boys.

Mr. Ruben set the tray on the counter.

"Look, Mama, the swimmers are here." He wiped his hands on his big white apron. Mama Ruben smiled as she put the meat and cheese in the showcase. Mrs. Ruben was a pretty woman. She did not often say very much.

"Mama, I think we are feeding the next state swimming champions," smiled Mr. Ruben. He waved his hand to include the other swimmers who had just come through the cafe door. "I'll tell you something, boys. When you win that State Meet, you come in here. Mama and I will feed you like never before! You wait and see."

Felix kept his head down as he made a sandwich for himself. He wished his father would not fuss over his friends. They liked his mother and father. He knew that, but...

"What's the matter?" asked his father as he peered closely at the boys. "You are all so quiet. Are you just hungry?"

"No, Dad, it's more than that," Sarah replied. "I guess you were in the kitchen when the boys were telling us."

"Telling us what?" asked Mr. Ruben. "Someone is sick?"

"We're all sick about the news that we heard today," one of the boys said. "There's a little problem of money. The Center doesn't have enough money to send the team to the State Meet. We have to come up with some way to earn the money ourselves."

"Ahhh, that's the way it goes," sighed Mr. Ruben as he threw up his hands. "Money. Always money makes trouble."

Mrs. Ruben suddenly spoke from behind the cash register. "Wait, maybe everything is going to be all right. Where is the newspaper? Here," she said as she spread the paper on the counter. "Look, it's as if it had been planned for you. Read it."

The boys and Sarah and Mary gathered around the paper. Their faces broke into grins as they read:

Clean Up For You And Youth

The City Council today voted in favor of a plan to help clean up the city and help the youth. People of the city are asked to clean out all old paper, rags, bottles, and scrap iron.

Young people are asked to sign at The Center for pick-up work. Paper and junk dealers will be on hand at the weigh station on First Street and Fifth Avenue.

The Council hopes that merchants will donate the use of their trucks.

People of the city are asked to place junk to be picked up on the curb in front of their homes.

"Hey! This is great!" shouted Felix. "How much do you suppose we could earn?"

"Who knows?" replied Mrs. Ruben. "Maybe a little, maybe a lot. Whatever it is, it will be something."

"What do we use for a truck?" asked Mike.

All eyes turned toward Mr. Ruben. "Now, boys," said Mr. Ruben as he held up his hand and started backing away. "It is an old truck. I would have to think about a thing like that for a while."

"What's to think about?" asked Mrs. Ruben. "You tell the boys they can have your truck, Papa."

Mr. Ruben looked around for someone to help him. He saw in a moment that he would get no help from the young folks. He threw up his hands. "What can I say? You can have the truck, I guess."

There was a shout from the young people. "I'll tell my dad that you're lending your truck," said Budd. "Then he'll have to do the same."

"Hurrah for you, Papa Ruben," shouted Green.

Sarah hugged her father. "You're great," she said.

Mr. Ruben beamed as if the whole thing had been his idea.

Felix smiled at his mother. She might not talk a lot, but when she did... A thought about Sarah flashed through Felix's mind. "I'll bet if Mom had her way, maybe Sarah and Mike could go to the Mixer."

The door of The Del swung open. Chunker, one of the city's best and biggest football players, entered the cafe. Felix and Mike looked at each other. A look passed between them that made them grin and nod their heads. Both of the boys rushed over to meet Chunker.

"Welcome, Chunker, old friend," said Felix as he pulled out a chair for the big player.

"Yes, sit down and rest yourself." Mike patted Chunker on the shoulder.

"What will it be?" asked Felix.

"What's going on? What's the matter with you fellows?" Chunker looked puzzled as he asked the questions.

"Nothing, nothing at all," Felix replied. "We're happy to see you, that's all. You know, Chunker, I think you're about the biggest and strongest person I know."

Chunker leaned his head on one hand and tapped the table with the other. "Something is going on here," he insisted.

Mary entered into the fun of the moment. "Why, Chunker, you really are the strongest person I know."

"Keep talking, Mary," smiled Chunker. "Coming from you, it sounds fine."

"How would you like to go for a ride with us the day after tomorrow?" asked Mike.

"Sure, why not?" Chunker answered. "That's my day off. Where are we going?"

"Oh, around town," Felix told him.

"All right, tell me what it's all about. I want to know before I start in on that corned beef sandwich you're going to make for me. I don't want anything to spoil my big, beautiful appetite."

Everyone in the cafe laughed. "Nothing could spoil your appetite; not rain, nor hail, nor earthquake," said Mike.

Felix turned a serious face to Chunker. "I've never known the time when you didn't want to do a good turn,"he said to the tall young man.

Mary came to sit beside Chunker. "Here's your chance to do a really big favor, Chunker," she said with a smile.

"You tell him, Mary," sang out the boys.

Quickly Mary told Chunker about the swim team's lack of money. Next she told him about the clean-up plans.

"Look, see for yourself," Sarah said as she spread the paper on the table in front of him.

"Now I get it," Chunker replied after he had read the paper. "You don't want me. You want my muscle."

Mike shook his head. "That's not true. We thought of your muscle only after we thought of your sweet nature."

"Do you mean you expect me to help you all day and then give the money to the swim team? Me—a football player?" asked Chunker as he stood up and put his hands on his hips.

There was no answer. Chunker turned his head to look at one person after another. Then his eyes came to rest on Mary. "If you think I'm going to do that—well—you're right!"

"I knew you'd see it that way," Felix cried. "You're full of good deeds, Chunker. Now I am going to make you the biggest sandwich you ever saw." Felix went to the counter.

"I can just see the headlines now," yelled Green as he waved one arm through the air: "Football hero cleans up city all by himself."

"Yeh," said another boy. "Swim team in need calls upon football's strong man."

"Lay off, will you?" asked Chunker.

"Do you really think we can earn enough to do any good for the team?" asked Green.

"I don't know," answered Zapp. "We're going to have to try hard if we don't want to miss this State Meet."

Mr. Ruben had been enjoying listening to the boys. Now he said, "When everybody works, things come out all right."

"That's right, Papa," Mrs. Ruben replied. She led him by the arm toward the kitchen. "When everybody works."

A few minutes later Mike caught Sarah's eye. "Can I walk you home, Sarah?" he asked quietly.

She walked quickly to the back of the cafe and stood beside her mother. "Mom," she said, "Mike is going to walk home with me. We'll go right home."

"Better ask your father," Mrs. Ruben told her.

"But..." began Sarah.

Mrs. Ruben shook her head. "Ask your father," she said.

Sarah's face lost its smile as she slowly walked to the kitchen.

"Dad," she said, "Mike wants to walk me home. We'll go right home."

Mr. Ruben did not answer right away. Then he turned and looked at his daughter. "No, Sarah," he answered her. "You will come home with Mama and me."

Sarah knew better than to say anything. Her face turned pink. She bit her lip to keep back the tears.

"It is the best way, Sarah," her father said. He turned to go on with his work.

When Sarah returned to the counter, she kept her head down. Felix had seen what had happened between Sarah and Mike. He knew what his father must have said to Sarah. He wondered if she was going to cry.

Slowly Sarah walked to the place where Mike was sitting. She shook her head as Mike looked at her. Then with a firm step she walked to where Felix stood. "But I am going to the Mixer," she insisted quietly to her brother. "I am! Wait and see."

Will It Work?

Four boys and Mr. Ruben stood beside the truck in back of The Del. The air was full of the early morning hum of the city. Already the cooking aromas from several cafes were pouring into the alley. Mike, Chunker, Green, and Felix stood beside Mr. Ruben as he made a last-minute check of the old truck.

"I think she will work, boys," Mr. Ruben said.

"It's pretty great of you to lend us your truck." Mike spoke for all the boys.

Mr. Ruben patted Mike's shoulder. "So the truck just sits here all day. Why shouldn't I let you use it?"

"He likes me," thought Mike. "If only he weren't so funny about letting Sarah go anywhere with me."

"You be careful, Felix," Mr. Ruben told his son.

Felix nodded. "Don't worry, Dad. We don't want to put any scratches on her. Climb in, everybody," he called to the other boys.

Mike climbed into the cab beside Felix. Chunker and Green scrambled into the back.

"Ready back here," shouted Chunker. The boys waved to Mr. Ruben as he watched them pull away from The Del.

"Where's the map of our streets?" asked Mike. The town had been divided among the groups of young people.

"You're sitting on it," laughed Felix.

Mike spread the map on his lap. "Turn here," he said when they reached a street which was lined with old houses.

Felix looked at the large old homes. "This looks good for our kind of work," he said. "There's old stuff in these houses if there's old stuff anywhere."

"Do you think people will really bother to set out their junk?" asked Mike.

"Oh, sure," replied Felix. "People are pretty nice—most of them, anyway. Besides, it's just good business. This way they won't have to pay anyone to have their junk taken away."

"I hope you're right," sighed Mike. "If we don't get to go...Look! There's a pile of stuff on the curb. It must be our first business!"

Chunker and Green jumped out of the back of the truck. "Back up a little," called Chunker. "Let's not carry this stuff any farther than we have to." He waved his arms to show Felix where to park. "There. Stop. Good. You'll make a fine truck driver someday," he said as Felix jumped from the cab.

"What do you mean, will? I'm a good truck driver already," answered Felix.

"Look at all that stuff!" Green exclaimed. "Do they still use old clothes for making paper?"

"Sure thing," Chunker said. "I read about that in some textbook. Look, here's a whole boxful of men's old hats." Chunker dusted off one of them. He put it on his head and pulled it down until it touched his ears. "Just fits." He turned to show the others.

Felix fairly dived into the box of hats. "What a find!" he cried. "I want one of those."

"Give one to me," shouted Green.

"Here's one for each and every one of you," laughed Felix. He passed hats to the others.

The boys shaped the hats to their liking and put them on. There was much laughing as they looked at each other.

"You are so good-looking," Chunker said as he looked at himself in the truck window.

"Stop talking about how beautiful you are and jump in," Mike shouted to Chunker.

They drove several blocks before they sighted another pile of junk.

"How come I do all the heavy lifting?" asked Chunker as they started to load the boxes. "All you fellows take is the little stuff."

"You should thank us for that," replied Mike. "Look at the good workout you're getting, and all for nothing."

"For nothing is right," Chunker complained. "But I don't want to be selfish. You boys need the body-building for the Swim Meet."

"Oh, swimmers are supposed to work on certain muscles only," Felix answered. He sounded very serious. "You know we can't do any shoveling or lifting of heavy things. It isn't that we don't want to do it. You know how it is."

"Yeh," Chunker agreed, "I know how it is." He reached for a huge box which seemed to be full of old papers. "Yikes!" he yelled suddenly. "A mouse!" The big box fell to the street.

Mike was the first to start laughing. Green laughed so hard that he fell to the ground on top of the papers, which were now sliding out of the broken box.

"A mouse!" shrieked Mike in the same way Chunker had.

"I don't see what's so funny," stormed Chunker. "It was a mouse and they can be dangerous."

Chunker's words started the boys laughing again. It was some time before they were able to stop. "Come on, fellows," Felix said at last. "Let's pick this stuff up."

At that moment an elderly lady opened the door of the house. She walked carefully down the sidewalk.

Felix lifted the hat from his head. "Good morning, mam."

"Good morning," the lady answered. "I heard some noise and I thought you might need some help."

"We're doing fine, mam," Felix answered. "We have lots of strong help here. We thank you for all the stuff you put out here, don't we, men?"

"Yes, mam, we do," agreed Mike.

"You're such nice-looking young men," the lady went on. "You young people are just wonderful."

Felix leaned over near Chunker, who was still grumbling about the mouse. "Be quiet. Do you want to hurt her feelings?" whispered Felix.

"What about my feelings? Nice junk! Huumph," he said.

The lady started back to the house. "Nice boys. Such nice boys," she said again.

The boys picked up the last of the papers and were about to get into the truck.

"Hey, look," said Mike. "She's waving to us."

"Take your hats off and wave to her," said Felix. He held the old hat over his chest and bowed.

The other boys did the same. "Wow, look at Felix," said Chunker. "What a businessman."

"You have to be nice to the public," said Felix.

"Yeh, business is business," remarked Chunker. "Isn't that what your dad says all the time?"

"That's right," agreed Felix. He knew his friends were teasing him again. Somehow he didn't mind today.

"What lovely junk you have," Chunker said in a voice that was meant to sound like Felix's voice.

"Let's go, you nice boys," called Mike. There was much laughter as the boys piled into the truck.

The boys traveled only a short way before they spotted more junk. They saw a box resting in the middle of a long driveway. Felix slowed the truck just as a man came rushing out of the old house. He looked over his glasses at the boys.

"Are you the ones?" he called.

"We're picking up junk, if that's what you mean," Mike called from the cab window.

"Stop right there, then," said the man.

"Yes, sir," answered Mike. Felix stopped the truck near the curb.

"Well, get out. Get out!" he yelled.

The boys jumped out of the truck and stood staring at the angry man.

"You see that stuff in the garage?" the man asked as he pointed down the long driveway. "Now I don't want you to back in the driveway. Driveways aren't made for trucks, you know. Trucks always leak oil."

Felix and Mike were the first to start toward the garage.

"Are you sure you are the right ones?" the man asked once again in a loud voice.

"We're the ones, all right," Mike answered.

"I do wish you'd hurry," complained the man.

"We will, sir," Mike answered. Under his breath he said, "Wouldn't you know that a fellow like this would have the longest driveway?"

"And the heaviest boxes," muttered Green as he lifted a box of dusty old magazines.

The man followed the boys part way on their trips from the garage to the truck. "The way you young people dress, a body can't tell if you're bums or not," he muttered. He peered at each of the boys in turn. "Young people aren't what they used to be. Always wanting a handout. What are your names?"

"I'm Felix Ruben, sir," Felix said. His face showed nothing of what he was thinking. "This is Mike Fisher."

"All right, all right," nodded the man. Felix wanted to talk to Chunker, but the old man followed him too closely.

"This is all of it," Felix called to the other boys. He picked up what looked like scrap metal. Two of the pieces were old fireplace andirons. "These are heavier than they look," said Felix. He bent under the load of the old iron.

"Close the garage door," yelled the man. "And don't leave any scrap on the driveway."

"Yes, sir," Chunker answered the man. "Thank you so very much, sir."

"Huumph" was the only answer Chunker received.

Mike raised his hat to the man.

"What did you do that for?" questioned Chunker.

"Business is business," answered Mike.

When the boys were safely in the truck, Felix pulled away from the curb carefully. "Whew! I'm glad there aren't many people like him."

"Me, too," said Mike with a shake of his head.

The truck had traveled only a few blocks when Felix pulled it over to the curb. "Why are we stopping?" asked Mike.

"There's something I want to look at," called Felix. He jumped out of the cab.

"Now what?" asked the two boys in the back of the truck as Felix swung up into the box. "Are you looking for a handout? Wasn't that guy something?"

Felix did not answer. He was looking for the old andirons. The others crowded around him as he studied them. "They're so heavy," Felix said more to himself than anyone else.

"I like that animal head on the top," Green said. He looked again at the andirons. "Could it be a lion's head?"

"You know what?" Felix said after a few more minutes of studying the andirons. "These might be worth something."

"Don't worry," Chunker laughed. "If they were worth anything at all, that old man wouldn't have given them away."

Felix was rubbing a spot on the iron. "They look very old. Say," he said, as he looked up from the irons, "I have an idea. We aren't very far from Grims's Old Treasure Shop. Mr. Grims knows all about old stuff. Anyway, Mr. Grims is a good friend of my father. It wouldn't hurt to ask him about these andirons."

The other boys seemed uninterested. "It wouldn't hurt to ask him," insisted Felix. "It'll take only a few minutes."

"You're the one with the nose for money," said Mike, "and it's your truck. Let's go."

Felix found a parking place a few doors away from Grims's Old Treasure Shop. "You fellows stay here," said Felix. "Old Mr. Grims might try to get the best of us if he thinks we all have a part in this. He'd never do my father out of anything, though. I'll hurry."

"Who would want to go in that dingy-looking place?" asked Green. "Did you ever see so much junk in a window?"

Felix started down the street toward the shop. "By the way," he called back to the boys, "you'd better put some money in the meter. I don't think we're supposed to park in that spot with a truck."

"You come back here," yelled Chunker.

Felix only laughed and staggered away with the andirons in his arms.

Chunker, Mike, and Green soon grew tired of waiting. They got out of the truck and stood beside the meter.

Chunker suddenly turned his back to the sidewalk. "Here comes Officer White," he said. "Who's got another penny?"

Green quickly slipped a coin into the meter. "Wait until that Felix gets back," he muttered.

"You're not supposed to be parked here, boys," Officer White said. "A truck isn't..."

"Oh, we'll be leaving in a minute," Mike promised. "We're on the "Clean Up For You and Youth" program. We just stopped here for a minute."

Officer White nodded. "Good work, boys. Looks as if you're doing all right. Just be sure to move out soon."

"We will," said Mike. "Oh, Felix, will you please hurry?" Mike said this under his breath.

Twenty minutes later Felix had not returned.

"What in the world can be keeping him?" Mike wondered.

"Do you suppose we should go in after him?" asked Chunker.

"No. Oh, oh! Look, here comes Officer White again," Mike whispered. "Put some more money in the meter."

Chunker quickly put a nickel in the meter. "Hey, here comes Felix. I just wasted a nickel," he added.

"Never mind," said Mike. "Get in the truck." Mike waved Felix a sign to hurry up.

Felix arrived on the run. "Sorry it took so long."

"Let's get out of here," said Mike. "Officer White told us twenty minutes ago that we couldn't park here."

"OK, I'll hurry, but wait till I tell you..." Felix was plainly very excited. He jumped into the truck.

"Save it until we get out of here," Mike asked. "Get this thing moving."

Felix backed quickly away from the parking spot. Chunker and Green waved at Officer White. He smiled and waved back.

"What happened in there?" Mike asked.

"As soon as we find a place to stop, I'll tell you," Felix promised. "I still can't believe it!"

Chunker was rapping on the window. Mike could not tell what he was saying. Felix pulled the truck over to the curb.

"Come on," Felix said. "I want to tell you all at once."

Chunker and Green were still sitting in the truck when Felix and Mike reached the back. "I'm not getting out here," said Chunker. "There's no place to eat."

"You'll forget about eating for once," Felix said. "Just wait until you hear what I have to tell you."

The Unexpected Happens

Felix seemed to be enjoying himself as he made the boys wait for his news.

"Tell us," begged Mike as the boys stood beside the truck. "How much did you get for those old andirons? I imagine you sold them. You don't have them with you."

"I didn't exactly sell them. Well—I did, in a way."

"What do you mean?" asked Chunker. "You sound as if you left your head in that shop along with the andirons."

"Would you believe I got five dollars?" Felix asked.

"Not bad," smiled Mike. "In fact, that's great!"

"Would you believe I got ten dollars?" Felix asked again.

The friends looked at each other. "Come on, now," said Green. "Tell us what you really got for them. Did you get one dollar—maybe?"

"Would you believe me if I told you Mr. Grims gave me fifty dollars?" Felix was almost jumping with excitement.

"Mr. Grims gave you fifty dollars?" Mike asked. His voice said plainly he didn't believe a word Felix was saying.

"He gave me fifty dollars—on account!" exploded Felix.

"On account of what?" asked Chunker. There was disbelief in Chunker's voice.

"Felix has lost his head," Green said.

"No, it's true," Felix answered. "Look!" He drew five ten-dollar bills from his pocket and held them out for the boys to see. The boys stared at the money. They seemed unable to say a word.

"It's like this," Felix began. "Mr. Grims gave me fifty dollars on account. He thinks the irons must be worth at least fifty dollars more. Maybe even more than that."

"I can't stand it," said Chunker. "Tell us what he said."

"Mr. Grims said I was very smart to have noticed that the andirons were unusual," Felix began. He stood up tall and smiled proudly at the other boys.

"Never mind that part," Chunker told him. "Go on."

Felix was not to be rushed in telling his story. "I told Mr. Grims I might want to shop around for a place to sell them. He told me that he could give me a better deal than anyone in town. Also, he told me he would never cheat one of the members of the Ruben family. He's going to ask another dealer about them—one that knows a lot about old iron like that."

"I can't believe it," said Chunker. "To think we almost sold them for junk."

Felix was not finished with his story. "I got to thinking how great it would be to hand Coach Burton the money today. I asked Mr. Grims if he'd give me something on account. I didn't expect fifty dollars. When he handed me that much, I just about couldn't keep from yelling."

"Do you know what this means?" asked Mike.

"Yeh, it means I'm going into the junk business," answered Chunker gleefully.

"It means that we can most likely go to the State Meet. Didn't you say there should be at least another fifty dollars?" asked Mike.

"Let's go and give it to Coach right now!" exclaimed Green. "Will he ever be happy!"

"Good idea," cried Felix. "Pile in and let's go. We can stop at the weigh station first. Then we ought to have even more than fifty dollars."

The man at the weigh station could tell that the boys were in a hurry. "Here you are, young fellow. You look as if you can't wait to go back for another load." He handed Felix several dollars.

"How about stopping for something to eat?" asked Chunker. "I'm starved."

"How can you think of food now?" asked Mike. "Come on. Coach must still be at the Center with the younger kids. Let's go tell him."

Coach Burton waved as he saw the boys coming toward him. "Going to get in a little extra practice?" he asked. "Hi, Chunker. Are you going to join the swim team? A little hard practice would be good for you football players."

The boys stood in front of the coach without answering. Each one waited for the other to speak.

"What's going on?" asked the coach.

"It's this," said Felix. He tried to make his voice sound matter-of-fact. "Here's fifty dollars." Felix held the money out to the coach. "And there may be more, too."

Now it was Coach Burton's turn to stand without saying a word. He stepped back as he looked at the bills that Felix pressed into his hand. "What bank did you fellows rob?"

All four of the boys started to talk at once. Finally it was Mike who told the story of the andirons. He finished by saying, "And you know Felix. He has a nose for money. He's the one who did it."

Coach Burton sat down on the bench by the pool. "All I can say is—Wonderful! But are you sure you want to give all this money to the swim team?"

"Why not?" asked Mike. He looked at the other boys. The thought of doing anything else with the money had not come into their minds.

Chunker laughed and said, "I almost wish I were a swimmer instead of a football player. Sounds as if you'll all be able to go, after all. You'll have quite a time."

"You sure are the right kind of manager, Felix," the coach said. He raised the fistful of bills overhead in victory.

Felix smiled, but something inside hurt. The coach must have seen the look on Felix's face, for he said, "You know what this means, don't you? It means that the whole team can go, but you would have been going anyway, Felix. You are going to break a minute before Meet time. The idea that you can't do it is all in your head. Do you know I can almost see you slow down after you make your turn? I don't believe it's because you're tired."

Felix looked down at his feet. What could he say?

"Your're in good condition," the coach went on. "You could go more than 100 yards. You have built some kind of wall in your mind. You aren't the first one to have something such as this happen to him. Sometimes, when we want to do a thing very much, we get so afraid we can't do it that we won't let ourselves go. I can't really explain how it is. That sort of thing is a little out of my line. But I do know this much. You can break a minute."

Mike, Green, and Chunker had walked to the door when Coach Burton began to talk to Felix. The coach followed Felix's eyes as he looked at the other boys.

Coach Burton said, "Those boys are your good friends, I've watched you. You worry too much about what the other fellows think and what they say. They like you. You know that. What if they do tease you about money or your curly hair? So what? Why do you want to be the same as everyone else? You'll never be the same and that's not bad. That's good. Look at me. I'm black. Nothing will change that and I wouldn't change it if I could."

"Yes, but you don't have to worry. You were—I mean you are a great swimmer," Felix said.

"You said it right the first time. I was a great swimmer, but I lived before that and I'm living after that. I wonder if you can begin to know the things I've been teased about. If people tease you about being different, be proud of it."

Felix ran his hand through his hair. "I am proud of what I am, I guess."

Coach Burton shook his head. "No, Felix. You can't 'guess' that you are proud. Either you are or you aren't. This country is strong because it has many people who are proud of being different from each other. It takes some folks a long time to realize that."

Coach Burton was watching Felix closely. No one had ever talked to Felix in this way before. He stood there unable to say a word.

Coach Burton was not finished. "You can spend a lot of time worrying about the fact that your hair is curly. I suggest you spend a lot of time thinking about how great your people have been in the past and how great they are right now. Your people and mine have both suffered. If we think only about that, we're wasting our time."

"I'm talking a lot, Felix," the coach went on. "What I want you to remember is this. Other people will like and respect you just as much as you like and respect yourself. You do a good job of pretending that you don't mind being teased about money and things. Start doing a good job of really not minding the teasing. Start being proud."

Coach Burton put his hand on Felix's shoulder. "You come to practice on Monday ready to be timed. We're going to get you over whatever it is that's keeping you from breaking a minute. Let's shake on it."

Felix smiled. "I'll be here," he said.

"Oh, and by the way," Coach Burton went on. "Thanks for being such a good man about money matters. I still can't believe we have all this money for the Meet."

For a moment Felix did not know what to think or say. Then his face broke into a grin. "Thanks, Coach," he said.

"I'll be seeing you," said the coach.

"Right," answered Felix. He ran to the door.

A New Hero?

Word traveled quickly about the 'find' that Felix and the three other boys had made. Several of the team members called Felix to ask questions about the andirons. What surprised the callers most was the fact that the swim team was going to get the money from them.

There was great excitement in the air at practice time on Monday. The boys gathered near Felix, Mike, and Green. Every now and then some boy would yell out loud just to show his happiness over the way things had worked out.

"How did you know that those andirons were worth so much?" asked one of the swimmers.

"I didn't," answered Felix. "I just had a hunch."

"Where there's anything to do with money, we'll listen to you after this, Felix," Budd said.

Coach Burton smiled as he entered the pool area and saw the excited team. "Pretty great, eh?" he asked. "But we can't stand around here talking. Now that we can take the whole team, let's get to work. Everyone in the water."

"Right away, Coach," Zapp replied. "There's one little thing we need to do first." Zapp looked around at the rest of the team members. They seemed to understand what his look meant. There was a quick rush of hands under Felix. Felix felt himself being swung into the air and over the pool. For a moment he was too surprised to understand what was happening. Then a rush of happiness flooded him. This treatment was something special. It was usually given only to coaches or captains of a winning team. As he hit the water and felt it close over him, he wanted to laugh and shout. When he rose to the top, the whole team was in the water beside him.

Coach Burton waited until the horseplay had quieted a little. He blew a blast on his whistle. "Now get to work," he yelled.

Felix felt lighter than he had ever felt in the water. He swam length after length.

"Hey, Ruben," shouted someone. "Can't you hear? Coach has been blowing the whistle."

Felix raised his eyes and saw Coach Burton waving to him to come to the end of the pool. Budd, Zapp, and Green were already on the blocks. "Oh, I forgot," he thought. "Coach said he was going to time the butterfly today. I wonder how long he's been waiting for me." He felt a little foolish as he pulled himself out of the water.

"Take a minute to get your breath and then let's go," the coach called to the four men on the blocks.

Felix took deep breaths of air. "I'm not ready," he thought.

"Take your marks," yelled Coach Burton. Bang! sounded the gun through the air.

Felix could feel that he had made a strong start. "It's good, it's good," Felix said over and over to himself as he glided under the water. Then all thoughts seemed to leave his mind. He felt strong. As he saw the far end of the pool coming closer, he knew that he was ahead of the others. He made the turn without really thinking about it. Every part of his body seemed to be working together in a new and wonderful way.

The air seemed filled with excitement. Felix did not hear the yelling from the boys. He did not see the team as he sighted the finish end. He could feel himself surge forward. Then he was there. His hands touched the edge of the pool.

There was a wild yell from the watchers. This time Felix heard the shouts. "You did it!" yelled someone.

Mike was down on his knees at the pool's edge. He was hitting Felix on the head. "59.4!" yelled Mike. "Do you hear that? 59.4!"

"Are you sure?" Felix panted.

"Yes, he's sure." It was Coach Burton who answered him. The coach was laughing as he looked at his stopwatch. "Do you know what you did? You made every one of these fellows better his time. Wonderful, Felix! Great work, everyone!"

Felix started to pull himself out of the pool. His arms felt as if they could not lift him. Somehow he managed to pull himself up. Coach Burton gave him a pat on the back.

Someone handed Felix his sweat shirt as he sat down on the bench. Felix looked up to see Zapp standing beside him.

"Nice going," said Zapp. "I couldn't catch you. I tried."

Felix smiled. Then he noticed that Green was beside him.

"I hope someday I can do what you just did," said Green.

"Thanks," said Felix and smiled again. "I must look like a dope," Felix thought. "All I can do is smile."

"Do you need a ride, Felix?" asked Zapp a while later.

"I sure do," answered Felix. As he bent to tie his gym shoe, Felix thought, "Zapp has never asked me to ride with him before."

"I ought to make you walk to wear you out," laughed Zapp. "I warn you, I'm going to do my best to beat your time."

A few minutes later Felix was seated in Zapp's car. He had never felt quite as much a part of the crowd. Soon there were six boys in the wagon and Zapp pulled the car away from the parking lot.

"I don't know if I would have given the money to the swim team or not if I had been you," one of the riders said to Felix questioningly.

"Yeh, how come you did that—you, of all people?" asked another boy.

There it was again—the same old talk about money. For a moment everything seemed to go black in front of Felix. Then something that the coach had told him pushed itself back into his mind. Felix laughed. "I guess I just didn't think about it carefully enough," Felix answered. "I admit it was a poor bit of business of my part."

By the time the car reached the street on which Felix lived, he had himself well in hand. There was something new about the way Felix listened to what the boys were saying. All at once he knew what that something was. For the first time he was really listening to what they said. He was not just listening for some remark directed at him. "I don't know how to tell anyone about this new feeling," Felix thought. "It's as if I had a raw spot inside me and it's beginning to heal."

Someone was talking to him. Felix came back from his own thoughts as the boy repeated his words. "I said, is that a police car parked in front of your house, Felix?"

Felix peered out the window. Yes, it was a police car in front of the apartment house. His family's car was there, too. That was strange. The Ruben car should have been at The Del.

"Maybe my dad has been speeding," said Felix. The boys laughed because they knew how slowly Mr. Ruben drove.

Zapp stopped the car in front of the apartment house.

"Maybe someone tried to steal all your money, Felix," laughed one of the boys.

"Let us know if anything is wrong," said Zapp.

"I will," said Felix as he crawled over the other boys. As he left the car, he added, "Thanks for the ride, Zapp. See you later."

The car pulled away from the curb. Felix saw the boys looking back at the apartment house. "I hope nothing has happened to Mom or Dad," Felix thought. He ran the last few yards to the door.

As he entered the hall, he could hear voices coming from his family's apartment. He could tell that some of them did not belong to members of his family. With a feeling that something was very wrong, Felix reached to open the door of his apartment.

Someone Is Lying

Slowly Felix opened the door into his family's living room. The first person he saw was his father. Mr. Ruben stood at the far side of the room. His face looked troubled. Mrs. Ruben stood with her hands twisted in her apron. Her face was very white.

"Oh, Felix," said Mr. Ruben as he rushed over to his son. "It is good that you are home. We have trouble." Mr. Ruben waved his hand in the direction of the couch, "You know Officer White, Felix, and this is Mr. Blackburn."

Officer White greeted Felix.

Mr. Blackburn pointed a finger at Felix. "That is the boy!" he shouted. "That's him. You took them!"

"Wait a minute," said Mr. Ruben. He stepped up to Felix and Mr. Blackburn. "I will do the talking, Mr. Blackburn. This is my boy. You will not call him a thief in this house."

For a moment Felix could not remember where he had seen Mr. Blackburn before. Then it came to him. He was the man who had made the boys carry the junk down that long driveway. He was the one who had talked about how terrible the young people were these days.

"Felix," said Mr. Ruben, as he looked straight into his son's eyes, "this man says you took his andirons."

"Stole them! is what I said," the man shouted. "He..."

"You be quiet," Mr. Ruben told the man. "This is my home and you will not say such things about my boy in this

house. We will let Felix tell how it was." Mr. Ruben turned again to Felix. "Do you know this man?"

"Sure, I remember him," Felix said as he looked at the man. "And I didn't steal anything from you. You gave us those andirons. They were in the pile of junk that you made us carry way out to the street."

"Why would I give you anything like those irons? I would have to be out of my mind to do a thing like that," Mr. Blackburn said angrily.

"Now, now," said Officer White. "If we can't talk this thing over without calling people names and getting angry, we'll have to leave. Mr. Blackburn, I didn't come with you to hear you shout at anyone. You said you just wanted to talk this over. I agreed to come with you because I knew both of you and I thought I could save everyone trouble. Now if you can't talk quietly, we'll leave. You can always handle this through the courts, Mr. Blackburn."

"No, no," said Mr. Blackburn. He leaned back on the couch. He seemed to be trying to control his anger. "I think it is better if we handle this here. All I want is my andirons."

"I don't have them anymore," said Felix.

"I know," said Mr. Blackburn. "I mean...well, I mean wherever they are, you can get them for me. Then I'll be on my way."

"Mr. Blackburn," said Felix. "You saw me carry those andirons away. You stood right there and watched me."

"That's a lie, you young...," shouted Mr. Blackburn.

"It's the truth, Dad. He saw us. You can ask the other fellows," Felix said to his father.

"I don't need to ask anyone else," Mr. Ruben said. "I know you tell the truth."

Mr. Blackburn was suddenly quieter. He smiled at Felix. "I don't want to make any trouble for you boys," he said.

"I only wanted to help. Now let's say there has been a mistake. You just get the andirons and bring them to me and we'll not have any trouble. I don't want to have to swear out a warrant for your arrest."

"I don't have the andirons and I don't have the fifty dollars," answered Felix. "I gave it to...never mind who I gave it to." The thought suddenly came to his mind that he must not get the swim team in trouble.

"How you get the andirons back is your business," said Mr. Blackburn. His face had a look that was meant to be a smile. "You can't go around stealing things, young man."

Mrs. Ruben had said nothing all of this time. Now she stepped forward. "Mr. Blackburn," she said in a voice Felix had never heard her use before, "I think it is better that you go now. My boy did not steal. I will not have you in my house saying that he did. We will talk this over and we will do what is right. We are honest people. When we decide what to do, we will let you know." Mrs. Ruben walked over and opened the door and held it open.

"Come on, Mr. Blackburn," Officer White said. "Sorry about this," he said to Mrs. Ruben as he went out the door. "We shouldn't have come here."

"You were right to come," Mrs. Ruben said.

Mr. Blackburn followed Officer White out the door. "I'll give you until..," he started to say.

"We will tell you when we have decided what to do," said Mr. Ruben. "We will do what is right. Goodbye."

"Such a business!" stormed Mr. Ruben when Officer White and Mr. Blackburn had left the apartment. "Calling my boy a thief. I could hardly listen to that man. Who does he think he is? First he throws something away and then he wants it back. Such a man!"

Felix sat down and stared at the floor. Suddenly all the good things that had happened lately seemed to be crashing around him.

"He saw me carry those irons out of that garage."

"Felix," said Mrs. Ruben as she came to sit beside him on the couch. "Felix, we know you are telling the truth. We believe you."

"What will we do?" asked Felix. "How do you suppose he found out that they were worth something?"

"He might have seen them in the window of Mr. Grims's shop," said Mr. Ruben.

"I can't just go and ask Coach for that money," said Felix. "I can't do that. The team is counting on it."

Mr. Ruben was walking back and forth in the living room.

"Besides," Felix went on, "they don't belong to that mean old man anymore."

"Now, now," Mr. Ruben said. "We will not be calling anyone names here."

"Mr. Grims is my friend," said Mr. Ruben. "We would have no trouble with him. We would give him fifty dollars and he would give them back to us. But there is more to it than that. "If we give them back to Mr. Blackburn, it is like saying Felix stole them when he did not."

"Dad, I can't tell the coach and the boys," Felix cried.

"If there is no other way, there is no other way," said Mr. Ruben.

"If we have to give them back, I'll work, Dad. I'll work and pay you back if you can only lend me the fifty dollars. I'll quit swimming and work and..."

"Does it mean so much to you, son?" asked Mrs. Ruben.

"Oh yes, Mom," Felix replied. "It means everything. I can't explain it, but...just don't make me ask Coach for that money!"

Mrs. Ruben nodded her head. "Then whatever we decide to do, we will not tell the coach and the boys. And we will not ask for the fifty dollars back. We will give the team the other fifty and you will work...that is, if we decide that is the right way."

"I do not think we should decide now what to do," said Mr. Ruben. "Who can think straight now?"

"You are right, Papa," Mrs. Ruben agreed. "Whatever we do must be the honest thing. It must be the way that keeps our son's good name for him. That is the most important thing we must remember."

"We could ask a lawyer or the police or somebody," said Mr. Ruben.

Mrs. Ruben shook her head. "No, we will think about it and decide together what we should do."

"Yes, Mama," agreed Mr. Ruben. "It must be what is right in our hearts."

Mrs. Ruben glanced at the clock. "Look, we have been gone from The Del so long. Sarah is there alone. After we work a little, we can think better."

Mr. Ruben seemed not to have heard his wife. "I tell you, Mama, I could hardly talk to that man. How did he dare come here and call Felix a thief? What I would like to do to that man! What a day this is!"

"Papa, Papa," said Mrs. Ruben. "You are getting angrier than when he was here. Come, we will go to work. Felix, you rest. It will be all right. Do not worry."

"I didn't mean to cause you all this trouble," said Felix, shaking his head sadly.

"Trouble," said Mr. Ruben. "How can you go through the world without trouble? What is a family for if not to stand together when there is trouble? Trouble will come. We will take care of it together. That is the way of a family."

Felix went to his room after his mother and father had left. He threw himself across his bed and stared at the ceiling, his mind awhirl.

"Why did I ever pick up those andirons?" he asked himself. "But if I hadn't, maybe the team wouldn't have been able to to decide what to do. I have to think of them and the coach. I'm sure the excitement made me swim better—I think. I'll never know if that was it or not."

In spite of the trouble, Felix seemed to have a warm feeling somewhere inside him. He couldn't quite decide what the feeling was. Then all at once he knew. His family had stood behind him. They had never wondered whether he was telling the truth. They believed in him. A family stood for something. He felt proud.

"They'll stand by me," he thought. "Maybe it's up to me go to the Meet. Maybe I wouldn't have broken a minute. and the team. It doesn't matter so much about me. If I don't give Mr. Blackburn the andirons, he'll make trouble. He might even get Chunker, and Green, and even Mike in trouble. If Mr. Blackburn makes trouble, the team might feel funny about using the money."

For a long time Felix lay without moving. His mind was busy. "It's up to me," he decided at last. "I'll ask Dad for the money to get the andirons back and also for money to give the team. That will be one hundred dollars. Then I'll quit swimming and work more hours in The Del. That way I can pay Mom and Dad the money back. It's the only way."

Slowly Felix got up from the bed. "The sooner I tell Coach that I have to quit swimming, the better," he thought. A half smile passed over Felix's face. "Coach said I was good at covering up how I felt. I hope I can cover up how I really feel when I talk to him."

Which Way Now?

"It's not fair, it's not fair!" burst out Sarah as she rushed in the door of the Ruben's apartment.

Felix had been about to leave. Sarah almost knocked him over as she ran into the room.

"Mom and Dad just told me about that awful man," Sarah cried. "Mike and Chunker and Zapp wouldn't steal. And everybody knows that you wouldn't."

Felix smiled, in spite of himself, at the way Sarah named Mike first.

"Thanks for not believing I'd rob a bank or something," Felix answered his sister.

"If you need some money—if you have to pay to get the andirons back, or something—I'll give you all that I have. Honest, Felix, you can have it." Sarah flung her sweater on the couch in anger.

"Thanks, Sarah," Mike said. "I think I'll have to get those andirons back and give them to Mr. Blackburn. It seems to be the only way to keep everyone out of trouble. I wouldn't want to get our names or my friends' names in the paper. I'm going to earn the money and pay it back to Mom and Dad. I got into this trouble and it's up to me to get out of it. At least the team will be able to go to the State Meet. I'm going to quit swimming and work more hours at The Del. That way I can pay..."

"Felix, you can't quit swimming. You must be crazy even to think of it. I just heard how you broke a minute today. You can't quit," Sarah cried.

"Listen, Sarah, it isn't the end of the world." Felix spoke quickly for he was afraid Sarah was going to cry any minute. "The important thing is that the team gets to go to the Meet. If I work hard, maybe by fall I can have the money paid back and I can..."

"No. There must be a better way. It's not fair for you to have to earn all the money. Besides, it may sound selfish for me to think about myself, but honestly, I've been so proud to have you on the swim team. I can't explain it, but it means a lot to me, too." Sarah looked most unhappy.

"Let's say it was nice while it lasted," said Felix. He was trying to pretend that leaving the team was not very hard for him. "That's the way things happen. Some people might say I'm a chump to care so much about what others think. But I don't want any trouble for the team or for me. There isn't anything in the world I'd hate more than to ask Coach for that money. I'd rather work all summer and all winter."

"Are you going over to tell the coach now?" asked Sarah.

"Yes, I might as well get it over with. I'm going to tell him that Mom and Dad need me at The Del. I won't be telling him a lie. They do need me. Every time I go to practice, it costs them money." Felix turned toward the door.

"I can't stay here," Sarah said. "Drop me off at Mary's house, will you?"

A few minutes later Felix parked the car beside Coach Burton's apartment. Felix could see him in the back yard.

"Hello, Felix," called the coach. "Did you come to help me with my garden?" The coach's garden had long been a joke among the boys. His plot was about six feet square. He was as proud of his garden as if it had been a large farm.

Felix tried to joke, but for once he couldn't think of anything to say.

"You look mighty troubled," said the coach. He began to scrape the dirt off his rake.

"Well, it looks as if I'll have to quit swimming," Felix blurted out to the coach. "It's been hard for my folks to let me have time away from The Del for practice. They need me and I want to help them. I'm sorry."

For a minute Coach Burton said nothing. Then he looked at Felix and said, "This is pretty sudden, isn't it?"

"Yes," stammered Felix. "I'm sorry..."

Coach Burton went on cleaning the rake. "Come on over here and let's talk about it," he said. He seated himself on the back steps.

"Believe me, I can understand your needing money," Coach Burton began. "But isn't there another way to work this out?"

"I don't know how," Felix said. He was finding it hard to look at the coach. If only he could tell the coach everything, but Felix knew better than to tell family troubles to others. "I can't talk about it," Felix went on.

"At least you won't quit until after the State Meet," said Coach Burton. "The team needs you."

Felix looked surprised. "You don't really need me," he said. "Zapp and Budd will do as well as I—maybe better."

"No," said the coach. "Winning a swim meet depends a lot on which swimmers are placed in each race. I've studied the times of the other swimmers in the state. I feel you could take the 100-yard butterfly and Budd might get a second place. This leaves me free to use Zapp in the backstroke, where I really need him. I was depending on you. I am still depending on you. In two more weeks your time should be even better than it is now. I hope there's some way we can work out a way for you to stay with us at least until the State Meet."

Felix was silent for a time. "It's funny," he said at last. "I never thought about the team really needing me. I was never good enough for that."

"Well, you are now," Coach Burton replied. "You should really try to find some way to keep swimming, Felix. You

have a future in this sport. When you cut loose the other day, I knew I was right about you. You could be a great swimmer. You have one of the best butterfly kicks I've ever seen. Not everybody has the body to butterfly, you know, but you do."

Felix was hearing words that he had wanted to hear for a long time. He shook his head sadly.

"Why don't you think about it, Felix? Talk to your mother and father. If you want me to, I'll talk to them," offered the coach.

"No, please don't do that. This is something I have to do myself," replied Felix.

"I don't want to make things harder for you. You've helped us so much with that money. Are you sure you don't want to use the money for yourself?" Coach asked.

"Oh, no, Coach, it belongs to the team," Felix insisted.

"I hope there is some way we can work this out so you won't have to quit," Coach Burton said as he laid a friendly hand on Felix's shoulder. "Maybe I'm being selfish. You think about it and do what you think is right."

"I will," promised Felix. "I'm really sorry." He felt as if he had just thrown away something very valuable.

Felix's mind was in a whirl as he traveled home. Whatever he did, he would be letting someone down.

Late that evening the Rubens were together in their living room. Usually when they were together, there was much talk. Tonight the four sat without saying very much. Finally Mr. Ruben said, "I do not think it is right that Mr. Blackburn should have his irons back. But I have thought about it and I see no other way to keep from having trouble. If we do not give them back, he will say Felix is a thief. He will make trouble for the boys. In the end we may have to give them back. Maybe he did not mean for you to take them."

"Dad, I know he saw us take them," Felix insisted.

Mr. Ruben held up his hand for quiet. "Yes, yes, I know, Felix, but always a person can make a mistake. We will find fifty dollars to give to Mr. Grims at the shop. Then we will find another fifty dollars and give it to the team. If you want to work and pay it back, that is the way it will be. I am not sure where we will get the money, but we will get it."

Mrs. Ruben nodded her head. "It must be that way. We must manage the money. Everything will stay the same with Felix and his friends. It is the only way."

For a long time that night Felix lay awake. "What shall I do?" he wondered. "Shall I wait until after the Meet to start working more hours at The Del? There isn't much left of summer vacation. I can't help Dad and Mom much after school starts, but how can I let the team and Coach down?"

Just before he dropped off to sleep, still another thought came to him. "Things will never be the same with my friends. I'll be out of things. They'll really tease me about money—if they bother to tease me at all."

By the time Monday morning came, Felix had decided that he could not let the team down. He appeared at the practice as always. The locker room was unusually quiet, even for an early morning practice. Felix wondered if he was imagining that each boy made a point of speaking to him.

"This won't last long," Felix said to himself. Then he was ashamed for having had the thought. "Why can't I just accept things as they are? Why do I always have to look for faults in what people say? I thought I was finally over that bad habit."

Everyone worked very hard at the practice. Coach Burton seemed in fine spirits. After a bad start, Felix was caught up in the excitement of it all and was soon laughing with the others. "Oh, if this could only go on," Felix thought. "I used to think practice was hard. Now I'd be happy to work even harder if I could only stay on the team."

After practice Felix hurried to The Del. Monday was a busy day. The Del had to be thoroughly cleaned. Felix worked very hard to help his parents.

It was nearly closing time when Felix noticed Mike's car in front of The Del. There seemed to be others with him.

"Sarah," Felix said quietly. "Mike's coming."

Sarah brightened and straightened her cap.

Mr. Ruben smiled as the boys entered. "You got here just in time," he said. "Mama, don't put everything away. We have hungry boys here."

"No, we're not hungry, Mr. Ruben. We know it's closing time. We only wanted to say hi to Felix," answered Mike.

"If you want something, I will be happy to...," continued Mr. Ruben.

"No, thanks," Zapp said, "but we might have some pop." Zapp and several of the boys went over to the pop machine.

The door opened and another group came in.

"Hi, boys," Mr. Ruben called to them. "What will you have?"

"Oh, nothing, I guess," one of them answered.

Mr. Ruben shook his head from side to side. "So many boys and not one is hungry. You are sick?" he asked.

"Mr. Ruben," Mike asked, "could we talk to you and Mrs. Ruben? It's pretty important."

"Now what is the matter?" asked Mr. Ruben. "Mama, come here, please," he called. He turned again to Mike. "I bet you want to sell me some tickets to something."

Mrs. Ruben smiled at the boys as she entered the room.

Mike looked at the other boys and then at Mr. and Mrs. Ruben. "We want you to know that we were with Felix when he picked up those andirons. He's telling the truth. That man meant for us to take them," Mike said.

"I believe you," Mr. Ruben said sadly, "but it does not matter. We have decided to pay." He stopped talking and looked at Felix and then at Sarah. "Who has been telling our family troubles to all the world?" he asked.

Mike seemed to be having a little trouble deciding what to say next. "It doesn't matter how we found out. We wanted you to know that Felix told you the truth."

Mr. Ruben suddenly looked tired. He sat down. "No, it doesn't matter how you found out. I thank you for coming. It is good that Felix has friends. But we believed our son. Felix does not lie."

Mike walked over to Mr. Ruben. "Here is fifty dollars," he said. He put an envelope in front of Mr. Ruben. "We know what Felix planned to do. We don't think it's fair for him to pay the money. We took up a collection and we got fifty dollars. Now you can get those old irons and give them back to that man even if he shouldn't have them."

There was no sound in the cafe. Some of the boys shifted from one foot to another.

Felix sat without saying a word. He looked as if he did not understand what Mike had said.

Zapp slapped Felix on the back. "It's all right, Felix, old boy. Don't look that way. Say something. I can't stand it when you don't have anything to say."

"I don't know what to say," said Mr. Ruben. "Oh, boys, you cannot do this."

"There's nothing to say," said Mike. "Except that now you can close up for the night."

At that moment the door opened and Coach Burton came into The Del. Mr. Blackburn and Chunker were with him.

"Hello, everybody," called the coach. "We were afraid you might be closed." Mr. Blackburn stayed near the door. He looked as if he would like to turn and go back outside.

Coach Burton reached back and took Mr. Blackburn by the arm. "There seems to have been a little mix-up, Mr. Ruben," Coach Burton said. "Mr. Blackburn has something to tell you."

Everyone in the room turned to look at Mr. Blackburn.

"Yes," began Mr. Blackburn in a quiet voice that did not sound at all like the one he had used in talking to Mr. Ruben before. "I was a little hasty the other day. I, well, I got to thinking. Maybe I made a little mistake. I mean..."

"Go on," Coach Burton said, "you're doing fine."

"Well, what I mean is, how would it be if we split the money we could get for those andirons? Maybe I never would have gotten around to taking them to a dealer."

For the second time that night there was not a sound in the room. Mr. Blackburn looked from one pair of eyes to another. "Well, I do think I should get at least something."

Mr. Ruben jumped to his feet. He went over to Mr. Blackburn and shook his hand. "I think that is fine! Just fine! I think we have no trouble. You are a better man than I thought, Mr. Blackburn. I am sorry for my thoughts about you. What do you say, Felix?"

Felix nodded his head. "Well, sure...," he said slowly.

"Yowie!" yelled one of the boys. Then others took up the cry. Some of the boys threw their paper cups in the air. Others hugged each other.

A grin spread over Felix's face. "You mean...?" he asked.

"Yes," laughed Coach Burton as he clapped Felix on the shoulder. "I mean you'd better get to practicing harder than you ever have in your life."

Mr. Ruben put an arm around Mrs. Ruben. "What do you think, Mama?" he asked. "Did you hear it? Mr. Blackburn is not so bad."

Mrs. Ruben smiled and wiped her eyes with her apron. "I think we will feed everyone now," she said. "We will celebrate. I will get busy in the kitchen."

Mr. Ruben waved his hand. "Everybody eats!" he said. "All our friends eat. On the house. You, too, Mr. Blackburn."

"Oh, Mr. Ruben, there's no need to feed us for free now," yelled one of the boys. "We've got money. Where's that envelope? Wow! Am I ever hungry." There was a dive for the money. The boys started to pass it back to its owners.

"We're rich again," said Chunker. "And I'm starved."

Felix started for the kitchen. "You go and sit with the boys, Felix," Mr. Ruben said. "Sarah and Mama and I will fix food for everyone. Sarah, you fix a big sandwich for Mike, and he will take you home." Mr. Ruben winked at Mike.

"Yes, Sir," said Mike. A big smile spread over his face. "Yes, Sir!" he said again.

Coach Burton sat beside Mr. Blackburn at the counter. The boys gathered around the big table.

Felix leaned over to Chunker. "Chunker, how did you ever talk Mr. Blackburn into...well, you know?" he whispered.

Chunker patted himself on the back. "You aren't the only business man in the crowd. We just had a little talk. Mr. Blackburn...well, it was all very businesslike. We pointed out some things to him, things such as how certain headlines could ruin a man's business. It wouldn't do to tell all our secrets." Chunker laughed. "Business is business, you know."

Felix threw back his head and laughed. He had never felt quite so wonderful in his whole life. "You're right." he said. "Business is business."

TEN FEET TALL
Howie Brown, an orphan, wants to be an athlete but finds that he is too short for most sports. He finds his sport in track. In the final meet he has a double reason for wanting to win. The closing pages of the book bring an answer to the mystery letters which Howie receives each month.

NO TURNING BACK
Tom Hoffman, a star football player, has good reasons for deciding not to play on the Center City team. However, he decides to play and accept the problems that he feels his playing will bring. Tom finds a surprising end to his problems.

FAIRWAY DANGER
Mike Fisher's love of golf and skin diving leads him into mysterious and dangerous happenings at Hickory Hills Golf Club. Mike's loyal friends, Bumps Blake and Chigs Moreland do some detective work of their own on Mike's behalf. A hospital stay for Mike brings an unexpected bonus.

TIP OFF
Chigs Moreland, star basketball player, hopes to win a sports scholarship to State University when a car accident takes him out of play. Center City needs Chigs to win the state tournament. Just as things are beginning to look better for Center City, Chigs makes a mistake which works another hardship on the team and a team member. Time almost runs out for Center City as Chigs tries to correct his mistake.

PITCHER'S CHOICE
Bill Weeks and his fatherless family share one dream. That dream has to do with baseball. Bill's pitching is not made easier by a man in a black suit who "rides" Bill at every game. A well kept family secret is "out" before some unexpected events change Bill's life.

FACE-OFF
When is breaking a promise the right thing to do? This question is one which Chet Lawson alone must answer as he works with his twin brother and the mystery man to turn a losing hockey team into a winning one.

SWIMMER'S MARK
Felix Ruben cannot seem to do the two things he wants to do most: improve his swimming time, and be accepted by all of the team members. Strange happenings make Felix a hero to the team members and at the same time threaten to keep him off the team.

TENNIS CHAMP
What happens when a girl must choose between pleasing her father and brother and doing what she believes is right? This is the question faced by Mattie Clark just as she is about to play in a long awaited tennis tournament.